Mrs. Gehrke

W9-BFF-894

This book is dedicated to
the loving memory of Rick Runyon,
who helped us all to fly.

Prepared in honor of Rick by Lisa, Julie and Marine

©2002 Jarrett W. Mentink, Ph.D. All rights reserved.

No part of this book may be reproduced, stored in a retrieval system or transmitted in any form or by any means, electronic, mechanical, photocopying, recording, or otherwise without prior written permission of the publisher.

Printed in Korea. First Edition.
ISBN: 0-9723314-0-9
Library of Congress Control Number: 2002094383

Published by Kids in the Clouds™
www.kidsintheclouds.com

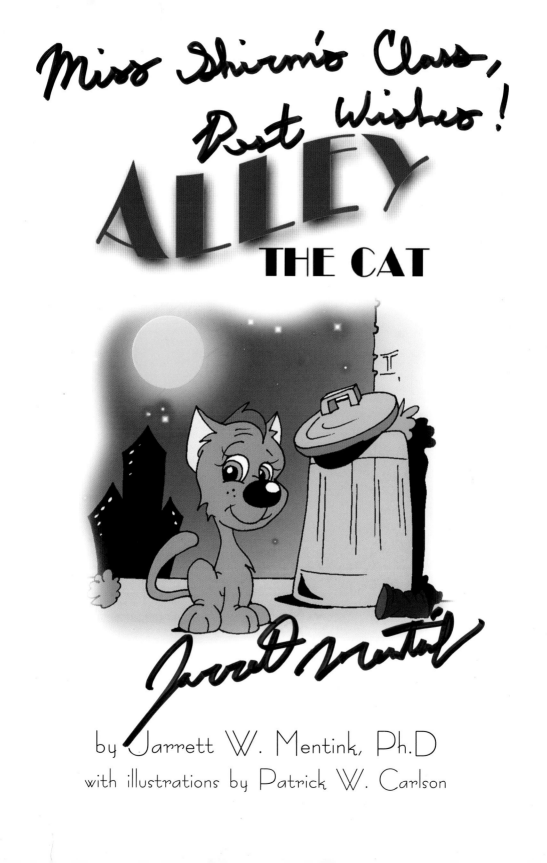

# ALLEY
## THE CAT

*Miss Shirm's Class,
Best Wishes!*

*Jarrett Mentink*

by Jarrett W. Mentink, Ph.D
with illustrations by Patrick W. Carlson

Our world has neat creatures,
some great and some small.
There are those that are tiny,
and those that are tall.

There are those with long noses,
and those with big feet.
There are those that are messy
and those that are neat.

Now most of these creatures
when you get them together,
Will get along great
like birds of a feather.

They will sing and they'll dance,
they will live side by side.
In fact, in some cases,
they will offer a ride.

But some of these creatures
just don't get along.
When they get together
things seem to go wrong.

Dogs don't like cats
and cats don't like mice.
They are often real naughty
and usually not nice.

But I know a story
that breaks this old rule.
I know of a cat
that mice find quite cool!

Her name is Miss Alley
and she lives in the street.
She has three roadside neighbors –
Skinny, Harry, and Crazy Pete.

Now Skinny is thin
just like her name,
And when mischief's at hand
she's likely to blame.

That brings us to Harry
with the large, bushy tail.
He likes to cause trouble
and does without fail.

The last of the trio
is the renowned Crazy Pete.
When it comes to a nutcase
he's hard to beat!

These three were the bullies,
the gang of the street.
They loved to chase mice
and when they caught them—They'd eat!

They had trapped many mice
and had many meals.
But there was one they couldn't catch—
The mouse nicknamed Wheels!

Wheels was a hero,
the fastest mouse in the land.
He ran like the wind
and his legend was grand.

He'd survived the three bullies
for a great many years.
He would run all around
and help save his peers.

Miss Alley would watch
as her three neighbors would chase,
Hoping to find Wheels
at the head of the race.

Miss Alley was different
than those other cats.
She liked all the creatures-
Even the rats!

Now Skinny and Harry,
and of course Crazy Pete,
Wanted Wheels most of all
for a fine tasty treat.

So the gangsters devised
a sneaky old plan,
To capture their mouse
and fry him up in a pan!

They waited for Wheels
to leave his small house,
Then let Skinny and Harry
start chasing their mouse.

While this was occurring
Crazy Pete played his role,
And pushed a big rock
towards the mouse hole.

Wheels was out running
away from his fort,
Taking cheese to his friends
and good things of that sort.

Skinny and Harry were no
match for Wheels' speed,
But this did not matter
since Crazy Pete did his deed.

He had taken that rock
and placed it at the front door.
When Wheels would come home
he could enter no more.

So as Wheels came a running
he hadn't a hunch,
That the gang was a smilin'
as they readied for lunch.

Miss Alley was watching
with such great despair,
Fearing poor Wheels
would be trapped in the snare.

As graceful as ever
Wheels arrived at his house,
But this day looked like
his last as a mouse.

Wheels screeched to a halt
when he came to his place.
His speed could not save him -
Not in this case.

He turned towards his foes,
those three hungry cats,
And his heart filled with sadness,
pitters, and pats.

Skinny, Harry, and of course
Crazy Pete,
Were licking their claws
as they readied to eat.

But just as they pounced
for poor, little Wheels,
The good ol' Miss Alley
made the greatest of steals.

She dashed out in front
grabbing Wheels by the tail,
And took him to safety
with all of her will.

The three cats were stunned
when they leapt for their dinner–
Poor, little Skinny would be
even thinner!

Miss Alley saved Wheels
so that he could run free.
She had taken a stand
for all creatures to see:

Out of her goodness
and kindness inside,
She had given a mouse
a friendly cat ride.

Miss Alley had shown them
in spite of the rule,
A strange looking creature
may actually be cool.

Some cats are Skinny,
Crazy or Harry,
And most mice will find them
to be a bit scary.

But in every cat family
there are those that are nice.
Some dogs like cats
and some cats like mice.